HOT WHEELS™

Drag Race!

By Ace Landers & Illustrated by Dave White

SCHOLASTIC INC.

ISBN-10: 0-545-11039-4
ISBN-13: 978-0-545-11039-6

HOT WHEELS and associated trademarks and trade dress are owned by, and used
under license from Mattel, Inc. © 2009 Mattel, Inc. All Rights Reserved.

Published by Scholastic Inc. SCHOLASTIC and associated logos
are trademarks and/or registered trademarks of Scholastic Inc.

12 11 10   12 13 14/0

Book designed by Henry Ng
Printed in the U.S.A.   40
First printing, March 2009

The drag race is about to start!

The racecars are different shapes and sizes.

There are trucks and cars.

There are skinny racecars, too.

All the cars drive fast!

The cars will race two at a time.
The track is short and straight.

The red truck is ready to race.

The orange car spins out its tires.

The set of lights is called a "Christmas Tree."

When the Christmas Tree
lights up, the race begins!

The light turns green!

The orange car and
the red truck take off!

The red truck wins the first race!

It ran the track in only seven seconds!

Now the red truck goes into the pit.

The mechanics check
the engine and the tires.

The next two cars are ready to race.

They are off!

Oh, no! The yellow car turns into the blue car's lane.

They almost crash!

The yellow car spins out!

The blue car is safe.

The blue car wins this race!

We have our two final racers.

The sun sets over the racetrack.

The red truck and the blue
car roll to the starting line.

The light changes.
Both racers hit full speed.

They are moving fast!

The blue car wins! We have a drag race champion!